Richard Rabbit Comes to Play

Peppa and George are
playing in their bedroom.
"Let's build a house,"
says Peppa.
"House!" snorts George.

Daddy Pig shouts up the stairs,
"George! Richard Rabbit is here!"

George's best friend, Richard, has come to play. George doesn't want to build a house any more. He wants to play catch with Richard.

"Hee! Hee!" squeaks Richard.
"Ha! Ha!" snorts George.

George and Richard start a new game. They turn the bedroom into Dinosaur Land. "Dine-saw!" roars George.

"You're too noisy," says Peppa. "And I've got no one to play with."

Mummy Pig invites a friend
over for Peppa. Now she has
someone to play with, too.

"George! Richard!" shouts Peppa.
"Suzy is here."
Suzy Sheep is wearing her
nurse's outfit today.

Peppa and Suzy
tidy up George and
Richard's toys.
"This is not Dinosaur
Land," says Suzy.
"This is a hospital."

"A hospital must
be clean and tidy,"
adds Peppa.

Peppa takes away George and Richard's dinosaurs. "These dinosaurs look ill," she says. "They must go to bed."

George and Richard gasp. "Dine-saw!"

"Shh!" says Suzy.
"Quiet in the hospital."

George and Richard
decide to play
something else.
"Choo-choo!
Choo-choo!"

The bedroom is not
a hospital any more.
Now it is George and
Richard's railway station!

Peppa and Suzy don't
want a railway station
in the middle of
their hospital.

"We don't like
little-children's games,"
says Peppa.

Suzy nods.
"We like
grown-up
games."

Peppa and Suzy get out the dressing-up things. Now the bedroom is Fairy Land!

"There aren't any trains in Fairy Land," says Peppa.

Suzy agrees.
"Only pretty things are allowed."

George and Richard burst into tears.

Daddy Pig and Mummy Pig run up the stairs.
"What's all this crying about?" they ask.

George and Richard don't like grown-up games.
Peppa and Suzy don't like little-children's games.

Daddy Pig has an idea. He takes everyone outside. "Look at all the muddy puddles!" he cries.

Snort!